d Fudge

The Loving Library

by Amandeep S. Kochar

PAW PRINTS
PUBLISHING
pawprintspublishing.com

Glossary
Bapu (baa-poo): *Dad* in Punjabi
Sewa (say-va): selfless service
Patka (pat-kuh): a piece of cloth that covers the head; worn by Sikh boys

Book and Cover Design by Maureen O'Connor
Art Direction by Nishant Mudgal
Illustrated by Weaverbird Interactive
Edited by Bobbie Bensur and Alison A. Curtin

English Paperback ISBN: 978-1-22318-354-1
English Library ISBN: 978-1-51826-300-2
English eBook ISBN: 978-1-22318-355-8

Published by Paw Prints Publishing
PawPrintsPublishing.com
Printed in Ashland, OH, USA

Jeet and Fudge love a good story.

Patka: a piece of cloth that covers the head; worn by Sikh boys

Reading is fun!

When reading, you never feel alone.

Sometimes, though, you can feel frustrated.

Like Jeet does when he can't sound out a word on the first try.

Fudge is patient.
She waits for him
to get it right.

She believes in Jeet!

Jeet would love to have more friends who'd like to read with him.

Friends like Fudge.

One day, Jeet sees a little boy on TV.

Bapu: *Dad* in Punjabi

"Bapu, why does he have all those books?" Jeet asks Dad.

"It's his sewa," Dad tells him. "He is donating books to children who are sick.

Sewa: selfless service

He also created a place in his town where people can borrow books for free."

"Like a library?" says Jeet.
"Yes," says Dad. "His loving library."

Then Jeet has an idea!

He and Fudge find their red wagon.

They take a walk with Dad.
They knock on one neighbor's
door. . .

and another. . .

and another. . .

and another. . .

while Mom
makes a call.

Then they all hang posters together, everywhere they can.

A few days pass. . .
They are ready for the big reveal!

ANIMAL SHELTER

"Wow!" says Jeet. "So many kind people donated books for our Loving Library!"

"Hello," says one little boy.
"I'm Jamal. This is Tugboat.
We'd like to grab that book!"

Yes! A new friend who loves to read!

Now Jeet and Jamal love to read together all the time. . .

with Fudge and Tugboat, of course.

And their neighbors too!

Even for the neighbors who can't make it to the loving library. . .

the four forever friends find a
way to deliver love and books.

Dear Reader,

Hello! My name is Anaik (rhymes with Drake 😊). I am ten years old. I love the Jeet and Fudge series because Jeet looks and acts like me, and because my project, Loving Library, inspired this book!

Loving Library is a nonprofit program that provides free books to people in need, including those in underserved communities. I started Loving Library because my grandma was hospitalized with COVID-19, and she was lonely. Reading makes me happy and helps to pass the time. I figured it would do the same for her. And it did! It made her feel a lot better. Now books that have been donated through Loving Library help people *all over the world* feel a lot better too.

You can help me provide books for those in need by visiting my website, lovinglibrary.org, and donating, or by volunteering to open up your own chapter! You can also follow all my giving adventures on Instagram at @anaikslovinglibrary.

Before I go, you may be wondering why I wear a *patka* (my head covering). Well, I belong to the Sikh faith, and it is against our religion to cut our hair. My patka protects my uncut hair. My hair and patka represent my commitment to treating everyone equally and doing *sewa. Sewa* is pronounced "Say-va," and it means to help those in need without expecting anything in return. It is one of the main values of Sikhism.

Thank you for your support!

Love,
Anaik